The Three Little Wolves

AND THE

Big Bad Boar

CLAUS KOCH

authorHOUSE®

AuthorHouse™
1663 Liberty Drive
Bloomington, IN 47403
www.authorhouse.com
Phone: 1-800-839-8640

First published by AuthorHouse   2/16/2011

ISBN: 978-1-4520-5321-9 (sc)
ISBN: 978-1-4520-5323-3 (e)

Library of Congress Control Number: 2011901074

Printed in the United States of America

Chapter 1

The Big Bad Boar

Once upon a time, there was a mother wolf. She lived deep in the evergreen forest. She had three little wolves. The oldest little wolf had curly blond fur. His curls glistened every time the sun's rays peeked through the tall trees. The second little wolf had thick shaggy fur. It was bright red, like a robin's breast. The youngest little wolf had sleek brown fur. It made him look elegant.

When the little wolves grew older, they grew more curious every day. They liked to go exploring. They explored all the trees around them. They explored all the hills and valleys. It was not long before they had explored the whole forest. One day, they became so curious that they decided to explore the world. So the little wolves said good-bye to their mother. They set out on the narrow path that led out of the forest.

The little wolves wandered for a long, long time. Finally, the path opened into the lovely countryside. There were many fields with different crops. There were rolling meadows. Pink clover blossoms covered some of them. Bees were buzzing all around. The bees were collecting nectar from the blossoms to make honey. The little wolves liked honey, but they were too afraid of the bees to take any of it.

The little wolves walked a while in the countryside. Soon they came to a small, wooden bridge. The little bridge crossed a small babbling brook. The oldest little wolf bent down and listened to the brook. He thought that it was saying something to him. This made the blond wolf very curious. He said to his brothers, "I want to follow this talking stream." So the younger wolves wished their brother good luck and continued along the path.

The blond little wolf followed the stream through fields of fragrant clover blossoms. He liked the countryside very much. There were pretty white daisies to sniff. There were busy bees to watch. There were big, sturdy trees to climb and many hills on which he could play. Some trees had ripe apples; some trees grew delicious walnuts. The little wolf tried something from each tree. For dessert, he picked some wild strawberries that grew along the stream.

After his delicious meal, the blond little wolf followed the stream some more. Soon he came to a wheat field. The wheat was ripe. It swayed in the gentle breeze that blew over the field. The wheat stems glistened like gold in the afternoon sun. The golden color reminded the little wolf of his own blond fur. He fell in love with the golden wheat stems. He walked along the wheat field until he met a farmer. The farmer was cutting down the wheat. "Why are you cutting those pretty golden stems?" asked the little wolf.

The farmer replied, "I am cutting the wheat so that we can make flour from it. Then we use the flour to make bread."

"Oh!" said the little wolf. He knew what bread was. Then he asked, "What do you do with the golden stems?"

"Oh, that is straw," said the farmer. "We use it for making straw roofs for our houses."

"May I have some of that straw?" asked the little wolf.

The farmer smiled and said, "Why sure, little wolf. You may have as much as you want."

So the little blond wolf gathered enough straw to make a small hut. Then he found a pretty meadow near the forest. There were many daisies growing in the meadow. In the center of the meadow was a big, sturdy oak tree. It cast a long shadow in the afternoon sun. The little wolf built his straw hut in the shadow of the big oak tree.

He had just finished building his very own straw hut when a big wild boar came out of the forest. The boar was mean and very hungry. He saw the little wolf as the wolf ducked into the straw hut. The boar thought to himself, "There is my supper."

So the big bad boar walked up to the hut and said softly, "Little wolf, little wolf, open the door, and let me in!"

The little wolf peeked out and said, "Not by the hair of my chinny chin-chin."

"Little wolf," cried the boar, "if you don't let me in, I'll charge and crash your house down!"

The little wolf didn't budge. So the big bad boar backed up. He lowered his head. "Snort! Snort! Snort!" he puffed.

He came charging at the hut. But the little wolf was

smart. He watched the boar come closer. The boar was charging. Faster and faster! Closer and closer. Suddenly, the hut moved out of the way. The boar went charging by.

The little wolf had picked up the hut from the inside and moved it over just in the nick of time. The boar felt very foolish. This made him very angry. He turned around and shouted, "Little wolf, open up your door, or I will smash your house down!"

The blond little wolf peeked out again and said, "Not by the hairs of my chinny chin-chin!"

So the big bad boar charged again. He didn't know that the little wolf had moved the straw hut in front of the sturdy oak tree.

The big bad boar was really furious. He charged blindly for the hut. The little wolf waited inside. The boar was charging faster and faster. He was getting closer and closer. The ground was shaking.

Animals were running away. Birds were flying off. Still, the little wolf stayed inside. The boar's snout was almost touching the hut. Suddenly, the little wolf jumped out of the hut through the window.

Smash! Straw flew all around. The tree shook so hard that leaves fell off its branches. The big bad boar fell over backward. He hadn't paid attention to where he was going. He had knocked himself out cold on the big oak tree.

The little wolf carefully stepped up to the sleeping boar, who was covered in leaves. Soon a big bump grew on the forehead of the nasty boar. The bump grew and grew. Soon it looked like a long horn on the head of the boar.

The little wolf climbed up the tree to see if there was a village nearby. He spotted the farmer's village beyond the wheat fields. So the smart little wolf hurried to the village. He told all the people that there was a unicorn sleeping under the big oak tree in the meadow. Some people had heard a big bang, so they went to the meadow to see what was going on. When they saw the bad boar with the bump on his head, they all laughed. They agreed that he looked just like an ugly unicorn.

When the big bad boar woke up the next day, all the people and animals called him "the unicorn." His big bump never went away again. So ever since that day, everybody called the big bad boar "the unicorn" as a joke. This made the boar very angry. He became even meaner than before. He hated everybody who called him a unicorn. He blamed the little wolf for everything—and so, from that day on, the big bad boar hated little wolves most of all.

The little wolf soon built himself a new straw hut close to the village. The people liked the smart little wolf. He helped the farmers harvest the crops. He told the little children funny stories. And because he had golden fur and lived in a golden straw hut, the people called him "Goldy Wolf."

Chapter 2

A Wolf Whistle

The two younger wolf brothers had stayed on the path. They walked until the sun went down. Soon it got too dark to travel. So the two little wolves collected some hay for a mattress. They put leaves over the hay so that it wouldn't tickle. They found some moss behind a big maple tree and used the moss for pillows. Soon they were fast asleep beneath the bright, twinkling stars.

The two brothers woke up at dawn. The morning dew had left silvery drops on their furry faces. The golden sun peeked over the horizon and dried their wet whiskers.

The two little wolves were hungry. The red wolf stood up to look for something to eat. As he looked around, he saw a beautiful rainbow. It was on the horizon opposite the sun. The rainbow had many pretty colors. The color that the red wolf liked best was the outside color. It reminded him of the color of his fur.

The little wolves had always lived in the forest where trees blocked the horizon. They had never seen a rainbow before. The red wolf said, "I think I shall see where those pretty colors come from." So the two little wolves parted.

The red wolf walked past many fields. Pretty red robins were singing in the morning air. Along the way, the little wolf found some apple trees. But there were no apples on them. He also saw that the crops in the field looked poor. He wondered about that as he followed the rainbow.

After a while, the rainbow slowly disappeared. The sun was getting higher in the sky. The wolf was getting warm in his furry coat. At last he found a little stream. He dipped his furry paw into the stream and scooped up some cool water for a drink.

While he lapped the water, he saw some thorny bushes. They were growing by the stream. Deep inside the bushes were lovely red raspberries. The little wolf carefully picked some of the berries for a snack. His furry coat protected him from the thorns. He wondered who had eaten all the raspberries on the outside of the bushes.

The little wolf walked on. He saw more robins flying about. After a while, he began to wonder about all the robins. Soon there were more and more cheerful robins. The wolf's red fur reminded the robins of their own red breasts.

The little wolf was feeling very happy. He began to whistle a cheerful tune. The robins liked the music. They sang along as they followed him.

Late that afternoon, the little red wolf came to a village. By now, the sun looked like a big red ball on the horizon. This meant that the next day would be sunny.

All the birds went to sleep in the nearby trees. The little wolf was very hungry. Luckily, he saw a bakery. So the little wolf went to the baker. He asked the baker for some bread. The baker was very friendly, but he was also poor. He could only give the little wolf a little bit of bread.

While the little wolf ate his bread, he asked the baker why the fields looked so empty. The baker told the wolf this story:

"Many years ago, the village had eleven beautiful robins. These robins sang lovely songs to the villagers every day. The villagers liked the robins very much.

"One day, a handsome prince came to the village. He

liked the singing robins so much that he stayed here. He helped the farmers pick their crops. He showed the blacksmith how to make stronger plows. He taught the children how to read. Everybody liked the prince.

"Then one day, a wicked witch came to the village. She put a curse on the prince that made him very ugly. The curse could only be broken if the prince could kiss a beautiful princess.

"The villagers were very angry at the witch. They wanted to make the witch take back the spell. This made the wicked witch very angry. So she put a curse on the village, too. She cursed the eleven robins so they would lay new eggs each and every morning. This spell could only be broken if the robins ate nothing but pearls and jewels for a whole day.

"Soon there were more robins. In time there were many, many more birds. They ate the crops in the fields. They ate the apples on the trees. They even ate the berries off the bushes. Soon the people barely had enough to eat.

"The prince was very sad that the people had become so poor because of him. He decided to leave the village. He wanted to look for a lovely princess who might let him kiss her. We never saw him again."

The little wolf thought about the eleven enchanted birds.

Surely there must be a way to help these people. The baker could see that the little wolf wanted to help. He asked, "Little wolf, would you like to stay with me and help me in the bakery? I am getting older, and I could use some help."

The little red wolf was glad to stay with such friendly people. That night, he curled up beside the baker's warm oven. Early the next morning, he helped the baker to bake some delicious bread. He was just packing up some bread to take to the market when suddenly, he had an idea.

All morning, the little wolf sold bread at the market. He was very cheerful, and so he made many friends. When he met a farmer, he asked if the farmer could let him have some hay. The farmer told the little wolf of a big haystack at the edge of the village.

In the afternoon, the little red wolf went looking for the haystack. It was just where the farmer had said it was. There was also a sturdy red maple tree. It was perfect for climbing. The red leaves matched the little wolf's fur.

The little wolf grabbed some of the hay. He climbed up the tree and began building nests. All afternoon long he made many, many nests. All this time, he whistled happy tunes. The robins heard the cheerful whistling. They all came over and tried the nests.

Late that afternoon, the villagers came to visit the little wolf. They didn't know why he was making all those nests. They brought him some bread for supper. They also brought him some red cedar wood for a hut.

The little wolf thanked the people. He built his hut in the tree. He felt this was a safe place to build it because his mother had written to him about the scary unicorn that his brother had outsmarted.

The little red wolf had just finished the hut when the sun went down. He looked around in the dusk. All the robins were sitting in the lovely nests that he had made. He whistled them to sleep.

The next morning, the little wolf climbed from nest to nest. Soon he found a blue robin's egg. He put the egg into a pouch. Then he tied a lovely red ribbon to that nest. He searched on. Soon he found another egg. He tied a ribbon to that nest too. Soon there were eleven nests that had ribbons tied to them. This showed where the eleven enchanted robins laid their eggs.

The little wolf took the eggs to the village. Now, when
he sold the baker's bread, he gave each of the poorest people

one robin's egg for food. These people were happy that they had a little more to eat.

From that day on, the little wolf brought the villagers eleven blue eggs every morning. Soon there were fewer birds being born, so there weren't as many birds eating the farmers' crops. Now the crops could grow better. After a few months, the people were no longer so poor.

The people all liked the little red wolf who lived with the robins. But they didn't know what to call him. Finally, the baker thought of a name everybody liked. From that day on, everyone called the little wolf "Robin Wolf."

Chapter 3

Such Lovely Boots

The youngest wolf walked the farthest along the road. In the afternoon, he came to an apple orchard.

A farmer was picking ripe apples. He was tall and strong. His face and arms were tanned from working in the sunshine. The little wolf walked up to the farmer and asked, "Can I have a few apples? I have not eaten anything all day, and I am very hungry."

The farmer looked down from his ladder and said, "Why sure, little wolf, help me pick some apples. Then you can eat as many as you like."

This sounded like a good idea to the little wolf. He just loved to eat apples. Besides, his feet were getting sore from all the walking. So the little brown wolf helped the farmer pick many apples that day. As his reward, he ate some apples. He also kept some for the next day.

That night, the little wolf slept in the farmer's barn. There was a tall horse that looked very strong and fast. There was a fat cow that mooed a lot. There were many chickens, too, and a cocky rooster. The rooster didn't look very friendly. The little wolf thought that the rooster might be afraid of him.

The next morning, the sun peeked through the cracks of the barn. The rooster crowed "cock-a-doodle-doo!" It was so loud that he woke everybody up. The chickens began to cluck; the horse whinnied; sheep bleated. All this noise woke up the little brown wolf. He was hungry, so he ate a few of his apples. He put the rest into a clean potato bag. Then he set out again on the road.

The little brown wolf walked all day. He only stopped by a little stream for lunch. He ate the rest of the apples, and he drank some water from the stream. The stream reminded the little wolf of his brothers. He wondered what they were doing.

After lunch, the little wolf continued on his journey. As the sun was going down, it turned to a pretty red color. The little wolf was happy to see that. It meant that the weather would be nice again tomorrow. The red sun also reminded him of his second brother.

Before it got dark, the little wolf saw a big castle ahead of him. It had high walls and many tall towers. The big drawbridge was closed. Behind the castle was a village. The little wolf was very curious. He decided to visit the castle first.

He reached the castle as the last rays of sunshine disappeared. As he got closer, he noticed that the castle was all grown over with red and yellow roses. It looked lonely and empty. The roses looked lovely. They were closing up for the night, as most flowers do. The little wolf was excited about the roses. It was too dark to see properly, so he stepped closer. He got too close. "Ouch! Ouch! Ouch!" he shouted.

He had stepped on one of the thorns. His bare feet were really sore now. Slowly, the little wolf hobbled into the village. By the time he got there, all the lights in the houses were off. So the little wolf fell asleep in the marketplace.

The next morning, the little wolf was very hungry. His foot was still sore. As he looked around the market for something to eat, he saw a cobbler's shop. He thought, "That will be my first stop," and he limped over to it.

The cobbler was a young man. He had a hunched back and a crooked nose. There were scars on his face and arms. All of this made him look very ugly. But he was a kind man. He saw that the little wolf was hungry and that he had sore feet. So the cobbler said, "Little wolf, would you like to join me for breakfast? I do not have very much to eat, but I will share what I have."

The little wolf was so hungry that he hardly noticed how ugly the cobbler was. He gladly agreed. So the two had a pleasant breakfast. The little brown wolf did not judge people by their looks. Soon he and the cobbler were friends. This made the young cobbler very happy.

The cobbler had been lonely. Few people wanted to be friends with such an ugly man. He said, "Little wolf, if you stay with me and help me, I shall make you a beautiful pair of boots. I am a very good cobbler, but most of the people do not want to come into my store because I am so ugly. You look very elegant. If you sell my shoes, more people will buy them. Then I shall earn enough money to pay you for your work."

The little wolf agreed to this. Soon, the shop was very busy. Everybody came to buy shoes. The little wolf learned how to make beautiful boots too. The cobbler made the little brown wolf the most beautiful boots that anyone had ever seen. The little wolf wore these boots everywhere he went. Everybody talked about the friendly little wolf and his lovely boots. But they didn't know what to call him. Finally one day, somebody called him "Wolf 'n Boots." Everybody thought that was a great name. So that was what everybody called the little brown wolf from that day on.

Chapter 4

The Enchanted Castle

One evening, the cobbler and Wolf 'n Boots were eating baked beans for supper. The little wolf asked the cobbler about the lonely castle covered in roses. The cobbler told the little wolf this sad but true story.

"I am actually a prince without a home. My uncle is the mean king. He wanted me to collect many taxes from the people. He has the most beautiful jewels in the world. But he wanted more money to buy even more jewels. I refused to help him do this. I ran away from him instead.

"I traveled many days. Finally, I came to a beautiful village. In the village there were eleven beautiful robins.

They sang to the people all day long. I decided to stay in that village.

"My uncle was very angry because I did not collect taxes for him. He paid a wicked witch to put a curse on me. One day, she found me in the village. She turned me into this ugly man that I am today. There is a way to break the curse. I must find a beautiful princess who will let me kiss her. I have tried many times to meet a beautiful princess, but I can't even get close to one because I am so ugly.

"One day, I heard of the enchanted castle. There is supposed to be a beautiful princess sleeping in the castle. People say she has slept for one hundred years. They say the same wicked old witch put a curse on the castle long, long ago.

"I thought that a sleeping princess would not mind being kissed by an ugly prince. So I came here. For many years now, I have tried to enter the castle. But the roses are too thick. This is where I got all my scars from. Many times I have tried to cut a path through the roses. Each time the roses grow together again before I can enter the castle. I have made many strong boots to protect me from the thorns, but the thorns are too sharp. They go through the toughest leather. Soon I became a very good cobbler. I started a shop in this village so that I can live here. Maybe some day, I shall find a way into the castle."

Wolf 'n Boots thought about the cobbler's story for many days. Every day, he had a new idea of how he could help. Every time, he realized that his idea would not work. Then one day, Wolf 'n Boots received a letter from his oldest brother. The letter told of the many adventures of Goldy Wolf. It also told of the story of the unicorn. The very next day, Wolf 'n Boots received another letter. This one was from Robin Wolf. It told the story of the poor prince and the enchanted robins. That night, Wolf 'n Boots got a great idea. He knew it would work, but he needed the help of his brothers.

Wolf 'n Boots told the cobbler that he had found a way to get into the castle, but first he needed to visit his brothers. He said that he would be back soon. The cobbler did not believe that Wolf 'n Boots could find a way into the castle, but he wished the little wolf a pleasant trip.

The next morning, Wolf 'n Boots said good-bye to the cobbler. He walked along the path on which he had come. Finally, he came to the brook that the oldest wolf had followed. Soon, Wolf 'n Boots found his brother, Goldy Wolf. Wolf 'n Boots told his brother about the poor prince.

He told the story of how the wicked witch had turned the prince into an ugly cobbler. Wolf 'n Boots also told his brother about his plan to help the prince.

The next morning, the two little wolves went to the forest where the big bad boar lived. They looked for the boar all day. Finally, it was getting too dark to look any longer. The two little wolves had almost given up when they heard a loud snoring just over a hill. The two little wolves got down on their furry bellies. Carefully, they crept up the hill. There, just a little way ahead, were two wild boars. They were sound asleep under two mighty oak trees. They sounded like they were trying to outsnore each other. One of the boars had a big bump on his head. It was the nasty unicorn.

The two little wolves gathered some rocks in the darkness. Next, they crept up to the boars very carefully. Then each wolf climbed up one of the oak trees that each boar was sleeping under. Up in the trees, the little wolves felt safe. So they went to sleep for the night.

The little wolves awoke early next morning. The oldest wolf took a stone from his bag and carefully aimed it at the sleeping unicorn. The stone landed right on the unicorn's bump. "Ouch!" shouted the nasty boar as he woke up. He looked around and saw the other boar sleeping beside him. So the unicorn hit the sleeping boar. The sleeping boar woke up and asked, "What did you do that for?"

The nasty boar said, "You hit me first."

"I didn't hit you!" said the groggy boar. "You must have been dreaming. Go back to sleep."

So the two boars went back to sleep. Soon, Goldy Wolf dropped another stone on the head of the nasty boar. "Ouch! Ouch! Ouch!" shouted the boar. This time he really slugged the other boar!

But the other boar would not fight back. He said, "You must have been dreaming again," and he rolled over to sleep.

This time, Wolf 'n Boots threw a big sharp rock onto the sleeping boar. That did it! The boar had had enough of his nasty neighbor. Suddenly, both boars were fighting to the death. The whole forest shook. Other animals ran away. The oak trees were shaking. The two little wolves had to hang on so that they would not fall down. The boars fought and fought. Both were as strong as they were nasty. Neither boar was winning. The leaves were falling off the oak trees. The boars kept bashing each other. The wolf brothers were getting worried. Without the leaves, the two boars might see them. Finally, the unicorn won the fight. He stabbed the other boar with his bump just as if the bump was a long horn. The big bad boar was happy he won. He was also very tired and sore. So he left to go to a pond where he could lie down in the cool water.

After the battle was over, the two little wolves came down from the trees. They checked the other boar. He was surely dead. So the brothers skinned the boar with a very sharp knife. The boar's hide was so tough that this took them all day. The two little wolves left the forest in the darkness. They did not want to meet the unicorn on their way home.

The next day, Wolf 'n Boots thanked his brother and left with the hide. The hide was very heavy. Wolf 'n Boots had to stop many times along the way. Finally, he arrived at the village where Robin Wolf lived. Wolf 'n Boots told Robin Wolf of his plan to help the prince. Robin Wolf was glad to help. The story of the poor prince sounded familiar. He said, "I have just what you need."

Robin Wolf disappeared into the tree house. When he came back out, he was holding a bunch of feathers. He said, "These feathers come from enchanted birds. They have magic powers. They will make everything as light as a feather."

Wolf 'n Boots thanked his brother. That night, the two brothers told each other of their adventures.

Early the next day, Wolf 'n Boots headed for home. He finally arrived late that night. The cobbler was happy to see Wolf 'n Boots again.

The next day, Wolf 'n Boots asked the cobbler to make a tall pair of boots with the hide from the boar. The cobbler agreed. He spent many days making the boots. They were very, very tough. Finally, the boots were finished. Then Wolf 'n Boots sewed on the magic feathers. He tried the boots on. They almost jumped by themselves. They were very, very light.

Now Wolf 'n Boots gave the cobbler the boots. He said, "Here, try these on. They will help you get into the castle." The cobbler could not see how these boots could help, but he put them on anyway. When the cobbler had the boots on, he could hardly believe how easy it was to jump. He thanked the little wolf and leaped out the door.

Soon, the excited prince was in front of the castle wall.
Then he remembered the roses. He carefully stepped on

one of the thorns. The leather was tough. The thorns did not get through.

The cobbler prince took a big leap. Whoosh! He landed on the castle wall. The roses were up to his hips. They did not prick through the leather. Whoosh! The prince leaped to a nearby roof. Whoosh! He leaped again. Whoosh! And again, from roof to roof. Whoosh! Whoosh! Whoosh! Each time, he landed in roses up to his hips. Each time, the boots protected him from the prickly thorns.

Soon, the prince was in front of the tallest tower in the castle. That was where the beautiful princess lay sleeping. Whoosh! One last leap, and he was on the tower window. There, before his eyes, lay the most beautiful princess he had ever seen. She was asleep beside an old spinning wheel.

The prince entered the room. He stooped over the princess. He gave her a gentle kiss. At that moment, his back straightened. His face became handsome again, and the princess awoke and rubbed her eyes.

All around the castle, the roses shrank away. The only place they remained was on the walls for decoration. People in the courtyard awoke. Horses whinnied. Everybody in the castle came back to life.

The prince and princess fell in love at first sight. Soon, the whole kingdom heard about the awakening of the princess. They heard how the magic boots had made it happen. Many people were invited to the wedding, including Wolf 'n Boots.

After the wedding, the prince invited Wolf 'n Boots to live in the castle with him. Wolf 'n Boots, however, would not go. As payment for his help, he asked to have the cobbler shop and the magic boots. The prince was happy to agree to this. He made Wolf 'n Boots his personal cobbler.

The prince and princess lived happily ever after. Wolf 'n Boots went on to other adventures. With the magic boots, he could run very quickly and leap very high. Wolf 'n Boots went exploring every chance he got.

Chapter 5

I Want Some Boots

One day, the mean king called for his royal carriage. He wanted to check on his royal tax collectors. Besides, he had heard some wondrous things. He'd heard that there was a fierce unicorn that lived in the forest. He'd heard that a village had changed its name to Robinville. He'd heard that the villagers were becoming rich. They were hardworking people. Their crops were growing very well. They were all very healthy from eating lots of eggs.

Most of all, the king was curious about the old enchanted castle. People were saying that it was no longer covered in roses. They also said that a handsome prince married a beautiful princess from the castle. And magic boots made all this possible! Really? Such wondrous stories in his own kingdom? He would have to see these things for himself.

So the king got into his royal coach. He said to the driver, "I need more money from taxes. I want to go to Robinville."

The king's coach hurried all day and night. The next afternoon, it arrived at Robin Wolf's village. The hardworking people had just had their best harvest ever. They were celebrating in the town square.

The king saw how pretty the village looked. He saw how happy everybody was. He stepped out of the carriage in the middle of the market square. Then he said, "I have decided that you can pay more taxes. I need the money to buy more jewels. I want you to pay double the taxes next month. I will have my soldiers take all your crops if you do not pay the extra taxes." Then the king got back into his coach and rode off again.

The people were sad to hear about the taxes. They did not know what to do. If they paid such taxes, they would be poor again. Robin Wolf was also sad. He went back to his red maple tree. He sat there for a long time. He tried to think of a way to help the people.

The king's coach traveled on. Next day, the coach came

to the beautiful castle. The roses only grew on the walls now. They were blooming beautifully. The king was vain about his own castle, but he whispered to himself, "I have to admit it. I think this castle looks much nicer than mine." Of course, he didn't know that his nephew lived there now.

Next, the coach arrived in Wolf 'n Boots's village. The king looked out of the carriage. He saw a sign that said "Royal Cobbler." He said to himself, "I think this is where those magic boots were made."

He ordered the coach to stop. Then he marched into the shop. Wolf 'n Boots was just making a new pair of boots. He looked up as the king marched in. The king said in a nasty voice, "I want you to make me a pair of magic boots. I want to run and leap with them all day long. I want them to be as light as a feather. I want you to come to my castle next Friday. I shall have the guards drag you in if you do not come."

Wolf 'n Boots decided that he'd better agree. This was the prince's nasty uncle. He was very mean. So Wolf 'n

Boots bowed to the king and said, "Your Highness, I shall be there to make you a pair of magic boots. They shall be as light as a feather." The king was happy with this answer, so he left.

Wolf 'n Boots decided that he needed help once more. He put on his magic boots and raced off to find his brothers. When all three wolves got together, they formed their plan.

Soon, the week passed. The king was ready to call his guards. He couldn't wait any longer for his magic boots. Just then, Wolf 'n Boots and Robin Wolf came out of the nearby forest.

They walked up to the drawbridge together. Robin Wolf carried a large bag by his side. It was made of red feathers. In it were all the things they needed. The guards let down the big drawbridge. The two brothers entered the castle. The guard led them before the king. The king could hardly wait for his boots.

The two little wolves bowed before the king. Robin Wolf opened his bag and pulled out some hay. He gave it to Wolf 'n Boots. Wolf 'n Boots put the hay into a bowl. The king was curious. He said, "I wonder what that is! I think it looks like hay."

Wolf 'n Boots replied, "It is magic material for the boots."

Next, Robin Wolf gave Wolf 'n Boots seven robin's eggs. Wolf 'n Boots cracked them. Then he threw them into the bowl. "I want to know what those things are," said the king.

Wolf 'n Boots said, "It is magic glue. It holds the magic material together."

Then Wolf 'n Boots pulled a jar of black stuff from his pocket. He added some to fill the bowl. Then he stirred the mess. The king said, "I think that looks just like mud." He didn't know that's exactly what it was. Wolf 'n Boots told the king that it was special coloring.

Finally, Wolf 'n Boots asked the king to step near the fire. He asked the king to take off his shoes. The king agreed eagerly. Wolf 'n Boots brought the bowl of black guck over to the king. It looked vile. He began to spread a thin layer over the king's feet and legs.

The king watched quietly. He didn't know that the black guck was made from hay, robin's eggs, and mud. While Wolf 'n Boots smeared on the guck, he said to the king, "This is my secret formula. It makes the boots fit like a glove."

Robin Wolf pulled some feathers from the bag and handed them to Wolf'n Boots. Wolf'n Boots stuck them to the black guck. The king said, "I want you to tell me what those feathers are for, little wolf."

"They will make your boots as light as feathers," replied Wolf 'n Boots. Soon, the warmth from the fire made the eggs solid. Then the little wolf added more guck and feathers. Again he waited until the new layer hardened. After seven layers, Wolf 'n Boots said proudly, "Your Highness, the boots are finished."

The king stood up. He walked around. He leaped and bounced. He had to admit it. The boots were light. They were comfortable. He could leap higher than he ever leaped before. The king was very pleased. But he did not really want to pay for the boots. So he said, "I thank you for this fine gift, little wolf."

Wolf 'n Boots had expected this all along. He bowed before the king and said, "Your Majesty, I have kept my side of the bargain. I made you a pair of magic boots. Please keep your side of the bargain."

The king answered, "I will think about that if you tell me what you want."

"I do not want any riches," answered Wolf 'n Boots. "I only ask for a symbol of your generosity."

"I think that is a fine idea. I want to know what that symbol is," answered the king.

Wolf 'n Boots replied, "I would like one of the keys to your royal treasury."

The king roared with laughter. The guards laughed. Everyone in the king's court laughed. Finally the king said, "I like your boots, but they are not worthy of my treasures. I have the most famous jewels and pearls. I spent many years collecting them. I think they are much too precious for you!"

Wolf 'n Boots answered, "I do not want your jewels, Your Highness. I only want one of your keys for as long as the boots last. Then I will proudly go back to my village. I will tell all the people how generous you are. I will tell them that you gave me a key to the royal treasury for making you a fine pair of boots. I will have the key with the royal seal to prove it."

This sounded like a pretty good idea to the king. He was so vain and foolish that he believed Wolf 'n Boots. So he ordered the royal treasurer to give Wolf 'n Boots one of the keys. Then he said, "I want to remind you that you cannot get to my treasure anyway. I keep it in a tall strong tower. I have soldiers guarding it all the time. I will have your heads if you try to take one jewel from that tower."

The two little wolves nodded their furry heads and bowed before the king. Then the guards led the two little wolves out of the castle. They quickly disappeared back into the forest.

Chapter 6

The Chase Is On

That evening, the king was tired from running and leaping with his magic boots. He wanted to go to bed. He started to pull off his boots, but they would not budge. They were too snug. Then the king looked at them more carefully. He saw that the boots were peeling and cracking. The bottom of the boots were almost worn through already.

Well! The king was furious! He shouted to his guards, "I want you to find those two wolves and bring them here! I want my key back, and then off with their heads!"

As soon as the sun came up, many soldiers marched out of the castle. They were looking for the little wolves. They did not have to look far. The two little wolves had camped near the edge of the forest. So the soldiers arrested the two little wolves and led them back to the castle. They did not notice that Robin Wolf's feather bag was much fuller than the day before.

The soldiers and the wolves were getting close to the castle. Suddenly, Goldy Wolf came running out of the forest. He shouted, "The big bad unicorn is coming! The big bad unicorn is coming!"

The little wolf ran straight for the castle. The guards in the castle wanted to close the drawbridge, but the soldiers were still outside with the two little wolves as prisoners. Everybody was running toward the castle. They were running as quickly as their legs could carry them.

The unicorn was really the big mean boar who hated wolves. He could run very quickly. He kept catching up to the little wolf, but the little wolf was wearing the magic boots. Every time the boar caught up, the little wolf would leap ahead again. This made the bad-tempered boar even more angry. He charged faster and faster. Both of them ran so quickly that they arrived at the castle just behind the soldiers. The guards did not have time to close the gate. Goldy Wolf and the unicorn ran into the castle. Well! You should have seen the commotion!

Everybody was running in all directions. Everyone was afraid of the unicorn. The frightened soldiers ran away and left the two little wolves standing alone. So Wolf 'n Boots and Robin Wolf hurried to the tallest tower in the castle. They knew that this is where the royal treasure was kept.

When the little wolves got close to the tower, they saw the big fierce guards. The guards were blocking a locked door with a big lock. The two little wolves hid behind a hay wagon. Suddenly, Goldy Wolf and the unicorn appeared. They were running straight for the guards. The little wolf shouted, "Run for your lives!" The guards dropped their weapons and ran away. Goldy Wolf followed them. The unicorn followed Goldy Wolf. They all ran around and around the courtyard.

As soon as everybody had run away, Robin Wolf and Wolf 'n Boots came out of hiding. They ran straight for the door. Wolf 'n Boots took the king's key from his pocket. He stuck it into the lock. He turned the key. Click! It worked! Now both of them strained to open the door just enough to sneak in. Once they were inside, they closed the door behind them.

The little wolves ran up the spiral staircase—up, up, up, around, around, around. Finally, they arrived at the top. There, lying all about them, were the most beautiful jewels anyone had ever seen. There were rubies, diamonds, pearls, and many other beautiful jewels. Most of these jewels were paid for by the taxes of the people.

Robin Wolf opened his feather bag. He pulled out an enchanted robin. He took a pearl and showed it to the bird. The robin had not eaten all morning. He was so hungry that he swallowed the pearl in one gulp. Then Robin Wolf showed the bird the rest of the jewels. The bird began to swallow them too. Next, Robin Wolf pulled another robin from his bag. He fed the bird a pearl and showed it the other jewels. That bird started gobbling jewels too. Then Robin Wolf got out another bird and again another bird. Soon there were eleven enchanted robins eating jewels.

Meanwhile, Wolf 'n Boots went to the high window. He stretched on his high heels. Wolf 'n Boots tugged with all his might. Finally, the window creaked open. The wolves could hear shouting below. Goldy Wolf and the big boar were still chasing the guards from the treasury around in the castle.

When Goldy Wolf saw the open window, he knew that his brothers were finished. He stopped chasing the guards.

He scurried up the stairs to the high castle wall. The big bad boar followed. Goldy Wolf leaped to the top of the wall and stopped. The big boar started to lick his chops. He thought that the little wolf had given up.

Many people saw the two at the top of the wall. They shouted, "Look out, little wolf! The unicorn will eat you!"

The angry boar leaped for the little wolf. But Goldy Wolf was still wearing the magic boots. He jumped way up into the air over the boar. The big bad boar went flying past Goldy Wolf and over the wall. He tumbled down, down, down. *Splash!* The boar landed in the moat. The walls shook. The people shuddered. The water splashed all the way up the wall.

All the people cheered. They were happy because they thought that the little wolf had saved the castle from the unicorn.

Back in the treasure tower, Robin Wolf and Wolf 'n Boots ran down the circular staircase. They sneaked out of the big door and locked it. Then they sneaked through the streets to get out of the castle.

Chapter 7

The Escape

The two little wolves sneaked through the streets. They were looking for the drawbridge. They searched from street to street. Finally they saw the drawbridge. It was just across the courtyard. But it was closed!

The two little wolves sneaked along the wall. They hid behind a hay wagon that was next to the gate. The guards were all looking up at the wall. Goldy Wolf was up there. He was holding his hands together over his head to show that he had won. Then he looked over the wall. The unicorn was limping off into the forest, unable to understand how the little wolf had escaped again. Some day he would find a way to catch that wolf.

Goldy Wolf spotted his two brothers behind the hay wagon. He called to the guards that it was safe to open the gate again. The guards thought that this was a good idea, so they lowered the big, heavy drawbridge.

The two little wolves waited until the guards had their backs turned. Then they quickly sneaked to the gate. Just then, another guard who was looking for the wolves saw them. He shouted to the other guards, "Stop those wolves or the king will have our heads!"

The guards at the gate turned around just as the wolves were behind them. They scooped up Robin Wolf and Wolf 'n Boots before they could take another step.

Before you could blink an eye, they were in front of the king. The king was just getting over all the excitement. When he saw the little wolves, he jumped up in anger. He squinted his eyes and shouted, "I knew I should not trust you. I tried those magic boots you gave me, and they didn't last one day. I want my key back."

Wolf 'n Boots bowed before the king and said very softly, "But Your Highness, you only said you wanted magic boots so you could leap and run. You did not say they had to last long. Weren't the boots magical?"

The king looked at the two little wolves with a scowl.

"I admit that the boots were magical, but I also wanted them to last long." Then he shouted again, "I want my key back!"

Wolf 'n Boots asked, "Would you like me to make you another pair of boots that will last longer?"

The king growled back, "I changed my mind about those magic boots anyway. I didn't know how tired I would get from all that jumping." Then he shouted again, "I want my key back!"

This did not surprise Wolf 'n Boots. He had worn his magic boots a lot. He knew how tiring it was to run and jump so much. So Wolf 'n Boots pulled the key from his pocket. He bowed before the king. Then he handed back the key.

The king grabbed the key. Then he pointed to the two little wolves and shouted, "I say now, off with their heads!"

Two guards marched the wolves to the dungeon.

Next, the captain of the guards came before the king. Goldy Wolf was by his side. The captain of the guards said proudly, "Your Royal Highness, this is the brave little wolf who saved the castle from the fierce unicorn."

The king looked very impressed. He smiled and said,

"I am very grateful to you, little wolf. I shall grant you one wish for your bravery."

The king's smile disappeared as he said this. He was afraid that this might cost him something. But Goldy Wolf knew how stingy the king was. He bowed before the king and said, "Your Highness, I thank you for your kindness. I ask for only one small favor. You have just sent my two brothers off to the dungeon. They are hungry little wolves. It will cost you a lot to feed them. Please let them go, and let all three of us leave."

The greedy king thought to himself, "I think that is a very cheap reward. I won't even have to feed those wolves."

The king grinned from ear to ear. Then he said, "I am pleased to grant such a lovely wish." Then he shouted to the guards, "I want you to release those two little wolves. I don't ever want to see them again."

Soon all three little wolves were together again. They bowed before the king, and then they left the castle.

Chapter 8

A Happy Ending

While the three wolves were busy with the king, the eleven robins were eating many jewels and pearls. Soon they were so full that they could not eat another thing. They flew out of the window and back to their homes.

The three little wolves hurried back to Robin Wolf's tree house. They traveled for two days and two nights to get there. As soon as they got home, they spotted the magic birds. Robin Wolf climbed up to the nests with the red ribbons on them. He looked inside. There was a robin's egg in each nest as usual. He cracked one of the eggs. Sure enough! Inside the egg was a beautiful pearl. So Robin

Wolf took the rest of the eggs to the village and gave them to the people like always.

After a few days, there were many people who had some beautiful jewels. Soon everybody knew that Robin Wolf's wonder birds were laying gorgeous jewels and pearls. The magic robins kept laying their special eggs for many days, until they had no more jewels to lay. Then they stopped laying eggs. They became normal birds again. The spell of the wicked witch was over. Now they just sang their beautiful songs all day.

Soon the king heard of the gorgeous jewels that were in his own kingdom. He sent the royal jeweler to buy as many of the jewels as he could. The king was glad that he had just raised the taxes. Otherwise, he might not have had enough money to pay for so many jewels.

The people in the village were happy to sell most of the jewels to the royal jeweler. The jewels were so beautiful that the jeweler paid them much money. Soon almost all of the greedy king's money was used up to buy the jewels.

A few days later, the royal tax collector came to Robinville. The people gladly paid the extra taxes that the king wanted. After all, it was the king's own money. Besides, they still had some of the money left over. This was just in case the king decided he wanted even more money.

When the jeweler returned to the castle, he brought the jewels before the king. The king grabbed some of the jewels. He marveled at their beauty. He said, "I think those jewels are as beautiful as my own. I will help you to take them to my royal treasure tower."

The jewels had cost the king a lot of money, but he thought that the jewels were worth it. When he got to the room where all the jewels were kept, he noticed the open window. "I wonder why the window is open," he said.

Next he looked around. His eyes landed on the jewel box. He muttered to himself, "I thought I had more jewels than that."

However, the king was more greedy than he was smart. He never found out that he had bought his own jewels back. So he remained happy. The people in the village were also happy. They paid their taxes with the money that they got from the jewels.

The eleven wonder birds were happy. They no longer had to lay eggs every day, and they could sing all day again.

The three little wolves were happy. They had outsmarted the greedy king. They had broken the spell on the robins.

They had even taught the mean boar a lesson about chasing wolves.

But someone was not happy. The big bad boar was still sore from falling off the castle wall. He now knew that he could not catch the little wolves by chasing them. He promised himself that one day, he would get even with the *Three Little Wolves*.

The End